Kakadu Jack

Written by
Brenda Parkes

Illustrated by
Guy Parker-Rees

On Monday morning,
Molly Mack
went to the market
with a sunshade and a sack,
went to the market
with a sunshade and a sack,
and a parrot on her shoulder
called Kakadu Jack.

Kakadu Jack,
Kakadu Jack,
a parrot on her shoulder
called Kakadu Jack.

First Molly bought bananas
and put them in her sack.

"Beautiful bananas!"
squawked Kakadu Jack,
Kakadu Jack,
Kakadu Jack.
"Beautiful bananas!"
squawked Kakadu Jack.

Next Molly bought papayas and put them in her sack.

“Perfect papayas!”
squawked Kakadu Jack,
Kakadu Jack,
Kakadu Jack.
“Perfect papayas!”
squawked Kakadu Jack.

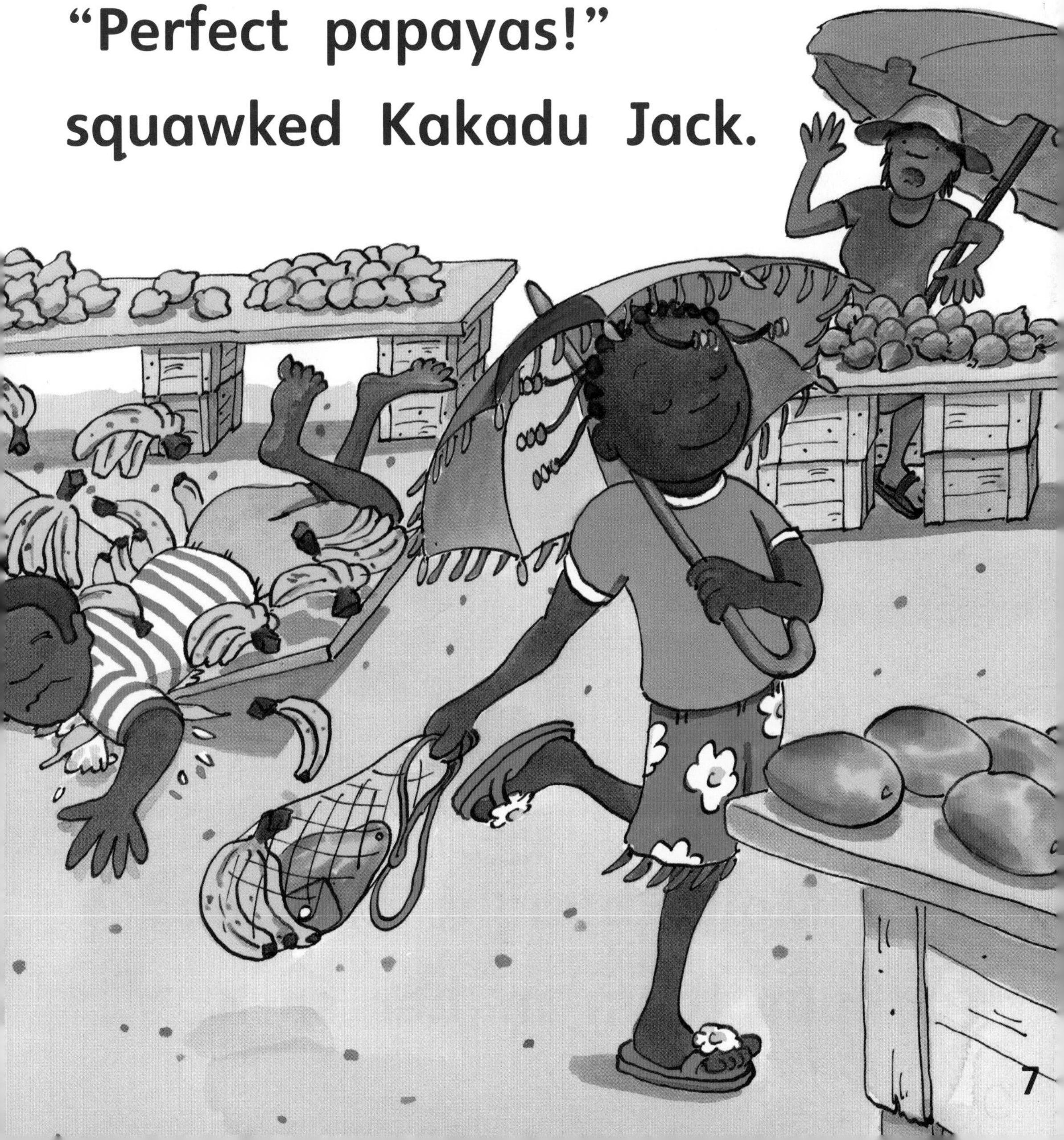

Then Molly bought mangoes
and put them in her sack.

"Marvellous mangoes!"
squawked Kakadu Jack,
Kakadu Jack,
Kakadu Jack.
"Marvellous mangoes!"
squawked Kakadu Jack.

Then Molly bought grapes
and put them in her sack.

"Glorious grapes!"
squawked Kakadu Jack,
Kakadu Jack,
Kakadu Jack.
"Glorious grapes!"
squawked Kakadu Jack.

Last Molly bought figs
and put them in her sack.

“Fabulous figs!”
squawked Kakadu Jack,
Kakadu Jack,
Kakadu Jack.
“Fabulous figs!”
squawked Kakadu Jack.

Later Monday morning,
Molly Mack
went home from the market
with her sunshade
and her sack,
went home from the market
with her sunshade
and her sack,
and a parrot on her shoulder
called Kakadu Jack.

Kakadu Jack,
Kakadu Jack,
a parrot on her shoulder
called Kakadu Jack.

“Did you like the market,
Kakadu Jack?”
“Yes! Let’s go back
tomorrow,
dear Molly Mack!”